W9-BHM-421

JPIC Meinde
Meinderts, Koos
The man in the clouds
WITHDRAWN $16.95
                      ocn756586597
1st U.S. ed.   07/17/2012

what you possess
is on its way
to others

WILLEM HUSSEM

Copyright © 2010, 2012 by Lemniscaat, Rotterdam, The Netherlands
First published in The Netherlands under the title *De man in de wolken*
Text copyright © 2010 by Koos Meinderts
Illustrations copyright © 2010 by Annette Fienieg
English translation copyright © 2012 by Lemniscaat USA LLC • New York
Translated by Claudius Translations, Dave Cooper & Vincent Janssen Steenberg
All rights reserved.

*No part of this book may be reproduced or utilized in any form or by any means, electronic
or mechanical, including photocopying, recording, or any information storage and retrieval
system, without permission in writing from the publisher.*

First published in the United States and Canada in 2012 by Lemniscaat USA LLC • New York
Distributed in the United States by Lemniscaat USA LLC • New York

Library of Congress Cataloging-in-Publication Data is available.
ISBN 13: 978-1-935954-13-2 (Hardcover)
Printing and binding ARC: Lightning Source, La Vergne, TN USA
First U.S. edition

The Man in the Clouds

Koos Meinderts & Annette Fienieg

The mountain has always been there. The man came later, much later. Nobody in the village down in the valley knew who he was, what his name was, or where he came from.

Suddenly, he was there, as if he had fallen out of the sky. But as soon as he settled down in his little wooden house on top of the mountain, it was as if he had always been there.

The man in the clouds, that's what people called him.

The man in the clouds rose precisely with the sun every morning, he opened his window and wished everything and everyone a good morning — the birds in the sky, the animals in the field, and the people down in the valley below.

He washed and shaved at the pump in front of the house, and on cold days, he lit the fire.

Then every day he sat in his chair and looked at a painting: a landscape so beautiful, so marvelously empty . . . this is what it must have looked like when the world began. You could see how everything was colored and shaped by the light of the rising sun.

The man in the clouds shared his happiness with anyone who wanted to make the climb. And there were many who did.

Every day you could see people coming up from below the mountain to see the man in the clouds and his splendid painting.

"Come on in,' he would always warmly welcome.

And there they sat, the people from the village. They silently looked at the landscape on the wall, and for a moment they forgot how gloomy and ugly life was sometimes.

When they had looked enough, they returned to their homes in the village in the valley; the man in the clouds gave a friendly wave. But as time went by they would return again to him and the painting.

Some people came more often, like the goatherd who was jeered and laughed at by the village children.

He came by very often. Just like the shell girl who stopped talking one day. And the old lady with a baby carriage and the doll she bottle-fed. And the man who always argued with the voices in his head. And the lonely boy who actually was a girl.

The man in the clouds didn't want anything in return, but he was very pleased when one day someone left a loaf of bread on the kitchen table.

Over time it became customary to bring him something: a chestnut, a rock, a piece of cheese, a marble, a bottle of wine, a feather, a song, or a drawing.

One morning the man in the clouds was busy stocking up his wood supply, when he saw a man coming up the mountain. It was a stranger stopping over on his way to town. He had heard the people down in the village talking about a man in a house on the mountain with a splendid painting.

The man in the clouds offered him a chair, but the stranger went straight to the painting.

'It's unbelievable!' he uttered. 'A masterpiece! Simply hanging from a nail in the wall! Do you have any idea how much you would ask for it?'

'Nothing, I don't ask for anything,' the man in the clouds answered. 'But most people bring me a little something. A marble, a feather, a song, or a loaf of bread, or a...'

'Sir!' interrupted the stranger. 'You have a fortune hanging on the wall! You have it made for the rest of your life! You're rich!'

The man in the clouds never looked at the painting in this way and he didn't want to look at it that way either. He wanted to look at it as he had always looked at it: a landscape so beautiful, so marvelously empty ... this is what it must have looked like when the world began.

The man in the clouds tried to forget about the
stranger, but something had changed. He still
welcomed visitors, but from then on he kept a
close eye on them.
He made sure they didn't stand too close,
or even worse . . . that they didn't touch the
painting.

He only received a couple of visitors at a time
and they were no longer allowed to stay as long
as they wanted. And one day, he showed
a visitor the door.

It was the goatherd (who had visited him the day before). The man in the clouds didn't want to see him any more.

And also that silly shell girl, and the old lady with her stupid doll, and the man who argued with the voices in his head, and the lonely boy who was really a girl. They might watch it until it crumbles!

The man in the clouds had a dream of thieves shouting: Hand over the painting immediately! That's how locks and bars ended up on his front door and why fewer and fewer people came to visit him.

Once in a while he thought back to the time when people from the village down in the valley came to visit him. They would enjoy the painting and bring him something in return: a marble, a feather, a song or a loaf of bread.

But those times were gone and he should not think about them. It was his painting, and he had to protect it, even with his life. He shut everything that could be shut even tighter and at night he slept with a chunk of wood under his bed.

He was startled awake by every sound. And one night he dreamed that right before his eyes the goatherd with the help of the shell girl and the lonely boy took the splendid painting off the wall and down to the village. At that point he decided to hide it.

From then on nobody was allowed to see his painting. To trick robbers and thieves, he continuously changed its hiding place. He became so good at hiding it that one night, he himself could no longer find it.

He turned his whole house upside-down and when he finally found it he doubted whether it really was his splendid painting.

He put the painting back in its old place on the wall and stood in front of it. He looked and looked and looked at it, but its shine had disappeared, its beauty was lost.

The man in the clouds took the painting off the wall, threw it in the fireplace and watched as it slowly went up in flames. He kept watching until there was nothing left of the painting but a pile of ashes. Then he removed the locks and bars from the door and opened the window.

He saw a landscape so beautiful, so marvelously empty
... this is what it must have looked like when the world
began. You could see how everything was colored and
shaped by the light of the rising sun.

Harris County Public Library
Houston, Texas